THE ELIJAH DOOR

A PASSOVER TALE

by Linda Leopold Strauss

illustrated by Alexi Natchev

Holiday House / New York

To Katie and Ryan, for bringing together
the Fentons and the Strausses
L. L. S.

For Simeon Venov "Mónata"—an artist and a friend
A. N.

ARTIST'S NOTE

The artwork for this book was inspired by traditional eastern European
folk prints from the eighteenth and nineteenth centuries. The artist
selected the technique of block, or relief, printing, first carving an image
into wood and linoleum plates using U- and V-shaped gouging tools and,
on some spreads, a magnifying glass. The raised surface of the plate,
which defines the image, was then inked with a roller and printed by
hand. Finally, each print was hand-colored with watercolor inks.

The publisher wishes to thank Rabbi Frank Tamburello
for his expert review of this book.

Text copyright © 2012 by Linda Leopold Strauss
Illustrations copyright © 2012 by Alexi Natchev
All Rights Reserved
HOLIDAY HOUSE is registered in the U.S. Patent and Trademark Office.
Printed and Bound in November 2011 at Kwong Fat Offset Printing Co., Ltd., Dongguan City, China.
The text typeface is Weiss.
www.holidayhouse.com
First Edition
1 3 5 7 9 10 8 6 4 2

Library of Congress Cataloging-in-Publication Data
Strauss, Linda Leopold.
The Elijah door : a Passover tale / by Linda Leopold Strauss ; illustrated by Alexi Natchev. — 1st ed.
p. cm.
Summary: A little help from the rabbi on Passover ends a feud between the Lippas and the Galinskys.
ISBN 978-0-8234-1911-1 (hardcover)
[1. Passover —Fiction. 2. Friendship —Fiction. 3. Jews —Europe, Eastern —Fiction.] I. Natchev, Alexi, ill. II. Title.
PZ7.S91245El 2011
[E]—dc22
2008049501

Many Passovers past, in side-by-side houses in a small village that was sometimes Poland and sometimes Russia, the Lippas and the Galinskys raised their children, pulled their beets, and shared their holidays almost as one family. For years the villagers had known that one day little Rachel Galinsky and David Lippa would marry and the Galinsky and Lippa names would truly be joined. But no more.

Now the families were feuding. The story told was this: Sometime last year, the Galinskys had swapped two fat geese for six of the Lippas' laying hens. Maybe seven. No one could agree on the exact number, but what was certain was that right after the swap, the two fat geese had died.

An accident, you might say. An act of God. Or had the Galinskys known their geese were sick? Had the Lippas insulted the Galinskys by asking for the return of their six (maybe seven) hens? Who knew? But sometimes in a small village, such arguments, however foolish, take on a life of their own.

Since the argument, Mama Lippa kept the windows of her house shut so she couldn't hear a single Galinsky voice.

Papa Galinsky cut a new side door in his house so he could leave for his shop without ever laying eyes on a Lippa.

Fortunately not all the Galinskys hated the Lippas, and not all the Lippas hated the Galinskys. David and Rachel didn't hate each other. And they thought it was horrible that this year, after all the years of joint Lippa-Galinsky Passovers, they couldn't have Seder, the special Passover dinner, together.

Rachel and David met secretly with the rabbi, who agreed to speak to their families.

"If you'd only sit down at the same table," said the rabbi to the Galinskys.

"The same table?" said Mama Galinsky, furiously chopping onions in her worn wooden bowl. "Never!"

"The children love each other," the rabbi reminded the Lippas. "They want to be together."

"Forget the children," said Papa Lippa, angrily mopping his brow against the heat in his closed-up cottage. "What about my geese? What happened to *that* Galinsky promise?"

The rabbi returned to Rachel and David, and the three of them made a plan.

"The neighbors will have to fib a little," said the rabbi. "Tell them I said God won't mind."

The next day, Mr. Schneeman the cobbler burst into Papa Galinsky's tailor shop. "Oy, Mr. Galinsky," he said. "Such a thing! Mrs. Schneeman hurt her wrist and can't even stir her soup! Could you find it in your heart to have us at your Seder?"

"Of course, of course," said Papa Galinsky. "Come both nights! You'll be our guests of honor."

"Ach, Mrs. Lippa," said young Mrs. Figowitz, walking up to Mama Lippa's vegetable stand and folding her hands appealingly over her large belly. "I'm afraid I'll have this baby in the middle of Passover dinner. Can I send Figowitz and the twins for Seder?"

"Of course, of course," said Mama Lippa. "Both nights. And you come too. If the pains begin, we'll all lend a hand."

One by one the neighbors came, with their "Oys" and their "Achs,"
to one family or the other, winking at David or Rachel, pleading
injury, poverty, bad planning, or broken dishes.

"Of course, of course," said the Galinskys and the Lippas. But where would they put everyone?

"Not to worry," said the neighbors. "We'll bring chairs. We'll bring tables. We'll bring chickens. We'll bring everything!"

Well, why not? Didn't the Seder service say "Let anyone who is hungry come and eat"? Mama Lippa sang as she aired the family's holiday clothes. Why, she felt almost sorry for the Galinskys, not being at this year's Seder.

Mama Galinsky, hanging starched curtains, could practically have cried for the Lippas. Would they have to celebrate all alone? But both women were too busy tracking down crumbs and banishing them from the house to think about these things for long.

As the sun slid lower in the sky on the eve of Passover, the village got ready for the holiday. In their respective houses, Rachel and David put dishes and fine cloths on the tables—two, four, six tables, across the floor, into the corners . . . and out the door.

Some guests would have to eat outside. Across their yards, the children grinned
at each other as the Galinsky tables approached the Lippas'. The plan was working.

"Rachel," called her mama. "Is the sun down?"

Rachel flew into the house. "Not yet, Mama," she said, dancing her mother away from the door.

"David," called his papa. "Are the guests coming?"
"They're still quite far away, Papa!"

And what was happening outside? In the space between the Galinsky and the Lippa houses, Rachel and David had been busy moving the tables of the two families closer and closer into one long, winding Passover table laden with silver cups and shining candlesticks and Seder plates. But the tables didn't quite meet yet.

And then, as the story goes, three things happened. First, the sun slipped behind the purple hills at the edge of town, sending up a bright star to announce that the holiday had begun.

Second, the Galinskys and the Lippas came outside to greet their guests and saw the tables almost joined. "Never," cried Mama Galinsky, but her voice held a quiver. "Over my dead geese," cried Papa Lippa (though no one was quite sure afterward what he'd meant by that).

And at that very moment the rabbi and his family rounded the corner, carrying chairs and embroidered pillows and the last holiday table, which they set down carefully between the Galinsky and the Lippa tables, joining the two together.

The rabbi placed the pillows on his chair and took a seat as David and Rachel slid in on either side of him.

"Dear friends, it's Passover," the rabbi said to the Lippas and the Galinskys.
"A time to celebrate the deliverance of our people from slavery. A time to
rejoice in our love for each other. We are all Jews, all family. So please . . ."

What could the Lippas and the Galinskys do? The rabbi was the rabbi.
And it *was* a holiday.

"*Baruch, atah, Adonoy,*" said the rabbi, lifting his wine glass.

"Wait!" cried Mama Lippa. Running into the house, she threw open her windows so the guests inside the house could hear the rabbi's blessing.

And then the two sets of parents sat down at their own places at the one long, beautiful Seder table and joyfully raised their glasses too.

Much, much later, when the candles on the tables flickered low beneath a sky full of stars, when the Four Questions had been asked and answered and the story of Passover told, when the festive dinner had been eaten and the

traditional middle matzoh hidden and found, it was time to open
the door for Elijah the Prophet, whose spirit visits all Jewish homes
Seder night.

Opening the door and feeling Elijah's presence on the breeze was David's favorite part of the Seder.

"But Rabbi," he cried. "How will Elijah know it's time now to come to us?" He looked at the tables filling the doorways. "The doors have been open all evening!"

"Except one!" said Rachel, grabbing David's hand and pulling him to the Galinskys' old front door, the one not used since the geese had died. "Go inside," she told David. "Unlock the door and welcome the Prophet!"

How the villagers cheered when that door flew open! After a few more prayers and songs, mamas and papas began carrying little ones home, leaving tables and chairs behind for the next evening's Seder.

And so began the tradition in that particular village that was sometimes Poland and sometimes Russia that every Passover, at one table, in two houses, with three doors, all the town's Jews gathered with the Galinskys and the Lippas in one great celebration of love and freedom and family.

And every year they welcomed Elijah the Prophet to their Seder through the famous Elijah door.